Time-Out from Technology
A Kid's Guide to Unplugging and Having Fun

Written by
Molly Wigand

Illustrated by
R. W. Alley

Abbey Press
St. Meinrad, IN 47577

Dedicated to
John, Joey, and Danny Jackson,
who help me keep my life in balance.

Text © 2015 Molly Wigand
Illustrations © 2015 Saint Meinrad Archabbey
Published by One Caring Place
Abbey Press
St. Meinrad, Indiana 47577

Library of Congress Catalog Number
2014959581

ISBN 978-0-87029-672-7

Printed in the United States of America.

A Message to Parents, Teachers, and Other Caring Adults

We see the warnings everywhere: too much time spent playing video games and watching TV places our children in danger of obesity, heart disease, and a host of other dangerous conditions.

As they grow into young adulthood, our children's relationship with technology becomes even more intense and complicated. The internet creates a dynamic in which it is difficult to discern which relationships are real and which are false or illusory. At a time when young people have more "friends" than ever online, the addictive technology keeps them from interacting with people in real life.

The media children consume on television and in movies is available on demand, creating an endless stream of content to be passively absorbed without ever leaving the house. Experts estimate that children ages eight to 18 spend an average of 44.5 hours a week in front of a screen. This overload enables a brand-new version of peer pressure in which children are judged according to their digital awareness and consumption.

While the burgeoning technology suggests some dangers to our children, there's no question it has benefits, too. We're living in a digital age, and to deprive our children of opportunities to explore and master technology puts them at a disadvantage as they progress in school and into the workplace. The ambivalent effects of technology on our kids make this a confusing time for families trying to do the right thing.

By establishing reasonable limits and nurturing an open dialogue with our children, we can help them become discerning and thoughtful consumers of digital media. We can implement parental controls and passwords to help set limits for children's time *on-line*. More important, though, is setting good examples by mindfully unplugging ourselves from the digital space and spending time with our kids *off-line*, providing opportunities for them to have fun and be stimulated by real-life experiences. This balance will help them become smart digital consumers who develop good habits and create healthy relationships.

—Molly Wigand

Technology. It's everywhere!

Have you ever stopped to think how much time you spend in front of a lighted screen? Whether it's a tablet, a computer, or a television, our electronic devices keep us company much of the time.

But there's more to life than all these screens! God gives us 24 hours every day, and it's our job to be careful how we spend them. It's okay to spend some time playing games, and watching movies and TV. But when we spend too much time hooked up to our devices, our lives get out of balance. We miss out on some of the amazing things the world has to offer.

Active or Passive?

We all have the ability to spend our days doing and being things that make a difference in our world. When you paint a picture or write a story or pick up your toys, you're making the world a little different (and better!) than it was before. You're being active when you're doing positive things like this.

But when you're watching a show or playing a video game for hours, you're simply taking it in. You're being passive. You're not using your mind and your strength to make or do something. And making and doing are two things that kids are really good at.

Get Up and Move!

Usually, we're sitting in one place when we're watching TV, playing video games, and surfing the internet. When we sit in one place, our bodies get out of shape. We don't get the exercise we need to be healthy and happy. Sitting around can make you tired, bored, and cranky, even when you're watching something fun on TV.

Just a little activity can improve your mood and keep your heart, lungs, and muscles working at their best! You could build a fun "walk around the block" break into your movie watching. Or do jumping jacks while you're waiting for your turn to play a game.

Grown-Ups Need Help, Too!

Sometimes the grown-ups in your life spend too much time looking at the glowing screens, too. If you're watching TV, and your dad is texting, and your mom's working on her tablet, it may feel like you're not together as a family.

If you think TV and computers are getting in the way of family times, have a talk with your mom or dad. God gave us families so we can love each other and share our ups and downs. Maybe your family can choose one hour a night that's unplugged time, or go somewhere and promise not to have your phones turned on. Don't let technology get in the way of being a close family.

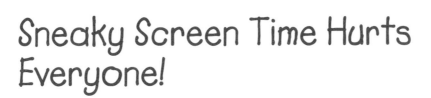

Sneaky Screen Time Hurts Everyone!

Sometimes kids keep playing games and watching TV after their parents ask them to go to bed. Other kids sneak computer or game time when they're supposed to be doing their homework.

Sneaking late-night video game time makes it hard for you to get enough sleep. It's easy to lose track of the time when you're playing games or looking at things on the internet. Chances are you'll stay up too late to do your best at school.

Your computer and video games should have a curfew just like you do. Follow your family's rules, and you'll be a happier computer user!

It's a Big, Beautiful, Unplugged World Out There!

When you've got your eyes glued to a screen, they're not able to see all the beauty in the world. Every day, spend some time outside listening to the birds, feeling the fresh air on your face, looking at the big sky, and taking in all the sights, sounds, and smells of nature. Right in your own neighborhood, hundreds of miracles are waiting to be discovered.

Nature is as amazing as any video game. You can make a list of all the birds you see and hear, or smell the pretty flowers that you find. You can look at the stars in the sky or catch a snowflake on your tongue.

Boredom Is Not an Option!

Some kids say that the reason they spend so much time playing video games and watching TV is that they're bored. The funny thing is that staring at the glowing screen and being passive can be a very boring thing to do!

If you're feeling bored, ask your mom or dad about joining a club, church group, or sports team. Another way to avoid boredom is to help other people by giving your time to visit a nursing home or clean up a park. These are ways you can make new friends, and that will make your life more fun, too.

Friends in "Real Life"!

Having friends online can be confusing. You may chat with people during video games, "talking trash" or just being friendly. It's okay to have friends in this way, but it's important not to depend on your online friends for all your conversations.

Be sure to spend time with your "real life" friends, too; you can't give a hug, hold hands, or play tag with your online friends. When you do make online friends, make sure your mom or dad knows who you're talking to. Strangers are strangers, whether they're on the internet or in real life.

Making Good Media Choices

While you're playing games or watching TV, you have lots of choices about where you spend your time. Some games, shows, and movies are especially for kids.

Some video games and TV shows have lots of violence, bad language, and other things that aren't good for kids. When you play games or watch TV with your mom or dad, they can help you decide if a show is OK for kids.

Try to find the kinds of shows and video games that make you feel good and happy inside. Listen to your heart. It knows when you're doing the right thing.

Friends Help Friends Do the Right Thing

It's always easier to do the right thing when you're making the decision about what to watch or play. But when you're at a friend's house, it may be a little harder to make good choices.

If your friend's parents aren't around and you find yourself watching something that feels wrong to you, you have the right to speak up. You can say, "I'm not comfortable watching this." Or, "My parents don't let me watch things like this."

A real friend will respect you for speaking up!

Too Much of a Good Thing!

How do you know if you're spending too much time playing video games or watching TV?

Think of playing on the computer like you think of ice cream. A scoop of ice cream once a week is a special treat. But if you eat ice cream all day, every day, it won't be a treat anymore. The same is true of computers, TV, and video games. If you play them a little, it can be lots of fun. If you play them all the time, they can make you bored, sad, and even sick.

Be Safe and Tell a Grown-up

Whenever you're online, whether you're chatting during a game or visiting a website, remember the safety rules:

1. Don't talk to strangers.
2. Make sure your parents know which games you're playing and websites you're visiting.
3. Never let people know where you live or go to school.
4. If someone makes you feel uncomfortable, tell a trusted grown-up.

If you're not sure which games, websites, or TV shows are okay, ask your parents. Talking about online safety helps avoid any misunderstandings and builds trust among all the members of your family.

Technology Helps Families

Most of the time, technology is a good thing for children and their families. Having strong computer skills is important and will help you get good grades and have a good job someday.

A movie night with your family in front of the TV can be fun. On the internet we can look up information about science and history. We can share our artwork, writing, and music, and we can learn about what's happening on the other side of the world.

Video games are a fun thing to do with our friends. Some games help us think logically about how to solve a problem.

It's All about Keeping Our Balance!

Growing up and learning to make good decisions about video games, computers, and TV is like riding a bike through a new neighborhood. We can discover exciting sights and sounds. We can learn new things about the world. But we keep our balance by doing what we know is right and staying close to the people we love and trust.

Our families can help us balance our time between real life and video games, TV, tablets, and computers. Together we'll find a way to enjoy the ride and manage technology in a way that's happy and healthy for everyone!

Molly Wigand is a writer and editor who lives in Lenexa, Kansas. She and her husband, Steve Jackson, have three sons. She is the author of a number of children's books and has taught creative writing to children and adults. She is a frequent contributor to Abbey Press Publications and is the author of the Elf-Help Book for Kids *Help Is Here for Facing Fear.*

R. W. Alley is the illustrator for the popular Abbey Press series of Elf-help books, as well as an illustrator and writer of children's books. He lives in Barrington, Rhode Island, with his wife, daughter, and son. See a wide variety of his works at: www.rwalley.com.